For Aunt Barbara and Uncle Don Larisey, who found
a spot on their rug and in their hearts for Deacon and Toby
—K. W. H.

For Pushkin, Buddy, Winnie, and Lucy
—D. S.

Henry Holt and Company, LLC, *Publishers since 1866*
175 Fifth Avenue, New York, New York 10010 [www.henryholtchildrensbooks.com]

Library of Congress Cataloging-in-Publication Data
Holt, Kimberly Willis. Skinny brown dog / by Kimberly Willis Holt; illustrated by Donald Saaf.—1st ed.   p.   cm.
Summary: Benny the baker sees no need for a dog in his life, but while his most faithful customer and the children who visit his bakery for
"Free cookie day" soon realize he has been adopted by a stray, it takes a heroic deed to convince Benny that the dog belongs with him.
ISBN-13: 978-0-8050-7587-8 / ISBN-10: 0-8050-7587-9. [1. Bakeries—Fiction. 2. Dogs—Fiction.] I. Saaf, Donald, ill. II. Title.
PZ7.H74023Ski 2007   [E]—dc22   2006009249

First Edition—2007 / Designed by Patrick Collins
The artist used acrylic paint, gouache, watercolors, and color pencils on handmade watercolor paper from India
to create the illustrations for this book. Printed in China on acid-free paper. ∞

10 9 8 7 6 5 4 3 2 1

KIMBERLY WILLIS HOLT

SKINNY BROWN DOG

illustrated by

DONALD SAAF

Henry Holt and Company

New York

NY'S BAKERY

CLOSED

Every day, long before the sun came up, Benny the baker walked two doors down to his bakery on Harmony Street.

MILK

He mixed the dough and made bread, cakes, cookies, muffins, and brownies.

Miss Patterson especially liked Benny's raspberry muffins and stopped by each afternoon at two o'clock to buy one.

Whenever a cookie broke, Benny placed the pieces into a box. Once a week he hung a sign in his window: *FREE BROKEN COOKIE DAY*.

After school, children hurried to the bakery to see if the sign was posted. If it was, they stopped in for a treat. If not, they waved at Benny and headed home. Benny looked forward to *FREE BROKEN COOKIE DAY* as much as the children.

One afternoon a
skinny brown dog
wandered into
Benny's Bakery.

"Sorry, but dogs aren't allowed in my bakery," Benny said as he led the dog outside with a warm piece of pumpernickel bread.

He does look thirsty, Benny thought. So he gave the dog a bowl of fresh water.

That night when Benny closed the
bakery, he found the skinny brown dog
still sitting outside his door. The dog stood
and wagged his tail
when he saw Benny.

He started to follow Benny home, so Benny stopped
walking. "Hate to break the news to you, fella, but
you're not my dog." Somehow the dog seemed to
understand and his tail pointed
to the ground as he
watched Benny
walk away.

Benny ate dinner, then sat
in his chair and read the news-
paper. He looked down at
the little rug in front of his
fireplace. It was big enough
for a dog. No, thought Benny.
I don't need a dog.

The next morning the skinny brown dog was sleeping outside the bakery. He awoke when he heard Benny unlock the door. The dog stood and wagged his tail, then started to walk inside. "Sorry, but a bakery isn't any place for a dog," Benny said again.

Benny gave him
a thick slice of
wheat bread with
butter and some
water. It was then
that he noticed
the small white
spot on the dog's
left ear.

At two o'clock Miss Patterson arrived for her raspberry muffin. The dog stood and wagged his tail. Miss Patterson dropped her purse. When the dog picked it up for her, Miss Patterson stroked the dog's head.

"You have a smart dog," she told Benny, "even if he is a little skinny."

"He's not my
dog," Benny said.
"Yes," she said,
"I can see that."

When the dog was at the bakery door the next morning, Benny shook his head, then noticed the dog's eyes. They were dark as chocolate chips. This time Benny gave him a bone with a little meat on it.

The children came by the bakery every day now even when it wasn't *FREE BROKEN COOKIE DAY*. They played with the skinny brown dog and taught him to walk on his hind legs.

When the children sang songs, the dog aimed his nose toward the sky and tried to sing, too.

Benny liked having the children around more often.

"What's your dog's name?" Sam asked.

"He's not my dog," Benny said as he slipped the dog
a broken gingerbread cookie.

"I think his name should be Brownie," said Pete.

The other children agreed that Brownie was the
perfect name for a skinny brown dog that ate and
slept at Benny's Bakery.

When Miss Patterson stopped at the bakery for her raspberry muffin, she patted Brownie's head and told Benny, "You have a good dog."

"He's not my dog," Benny told her every day. And every day Miss Patterson said, "Yes, I can see that."

That evening Benny turned off the bakery light,
locked the door, and went home. He wouldn't look
at Brownie as he walked away. But Brownie watched
Benny until he disappeared into his house.

Benny cooked dinner
and read the paper and
tried not to notice the
empty spot on the rug.

The next day, when it was too early for the children and even for Miss Patterson, Benny climbed a ladder to the very top and reached for a new bag of sugar.

On the way down his foot missed a rung, and he fell to the floor with a big CRASH!

Brownie came to the door right away, but
he wouldn't step inside because he knew
Benny didn't allow him in the bakery.

"Help!" Benny yelled. "Help me, Brownie!"

Brownie ran up and down the street barking.
People walked by, but no one stopped except Miss
Patterson, who was on her way to buy her raspberry
muffin. "What's wrong, Brownie?" she asked.

Brownie tugged at her dress,
pulling her toward the bakery.

When she stepped inside, Miss Patterson saw what was wrong. She rushed over to Benny and called an ambulance.

Soon the paramedics arrived. "It looks like you broke your leg," said one.

"It's a bad break," said the other. "You'll probably have to stay at the hospital a few days."

As they carried him to the ambulance, Benny asked Miss Patterson, "Who will take care of Brownie?"

"Don't worry," Miss Patterson said. "I'll watch him."

Benny had to stay in the hospital for a week. The first day Miss Patterson and the children came to visit after school. Benny was happy to see them, but he asked, "How is Brownie?"

So the next day the children called Benny's name
from outside his hospital window. Benny smiled when
he saw Brownie. Brownie wagged his tail when he saw
Benny.

"Can't they come inside my room?" Benny asked the
nurse.

"The children may," she said, "but a hospital is no
place for a dog."

"I don't see the harm in letting in one skinny brown
dog," mumbled Benny.

"I'm sorry," said the nurse. "Hospital rules." When she
saw Brownie twirl on his hind legs, she added, "Smart
dog, though."

Benny waved out the window and noticed for the first time that Brownie wasn't that skinny anymore. The children began to sing a song. Brownie joined in.

"You're a good fella, Brownie," Benny said as the children walked away with the not-so-skinny brown dog that had no home, but ate and slept at Benny's Bakery.

All week the children returned. Sometimes Miss
Patterson came, too.
"I sure miss your raspberry muffins," she told Benny.

"We miss *FREE BROKEN COOKIE DAY*," said the children.
"I miss the bakery," said Benny. "Especially Brownie."
Finally Saturday arrived and Benny went home.

This time,
Brownie did, too.